WITHDRAWN

A Moose That Says Moooooooooo

A Moose That Says Mooooooooooo...

Jennifer Hamburg

Pictures by

Sue Truesdell

Farrar Straus Giroux • New York

Farrar Straus Giroux Books for Young Readers
175 Fifth Avenue, New York 10010

Text copyright © 2013 by Jennifer Hamburg
Pictures copyright © 2013 by Sue Truesdell
All rights reserved
Color separations by Bright Arts (H.K.) Ltd.
Printed in China by Macmillan Production (Asia) Ltd.,
Kowloon Bay, Hong Kong (supplier code 10)
Designed by Anne Diebel
First edition, 2013
1   3   5   7   9   10   8   6   4   2

mackids.com

Library of Congress Cataloging-in-Publication Data
Hamburg, Jennifer.
    A moose that says moo / Jennifer Hamburg ; pictures by Sue Truesdell.
   —First edition.
        pages   cm
    Summary: "Chaos ensues when a child imagines a zoo filled with animals
doing the unusual and the unlikely"—Provided by publisher.
    ISBN 978-0-374-35058-1 (hardcover)
    [1. Stories in rhyme.   2. Zoos—Fiction.   3. Zoo animals—Fiction.   4.
Animals—Fiction.   5. Humorous stories.]   I. Truesdell, Sue, illustrator.
II. Title.

PZ8.3.H172Moo 2013
[E]—dc23
                                                                                2013000498

Farrar Straus Giroux Books for Young Readers may be purchased for business or
promotional use. For information on bulk purchases please contact
Macmillan Corporate and Premium Sales Department at (800) 221-7945 x5442
or by email at specialmarkets@macmillan.com.

If I were allowed to invent my own zoo,
the first thing I'd have is a moose that said "moo."

Next would come sharks that would read book after book.

An ox would serve eggs as a short-order cook.

The bears would drive cars.

The skunks would jump rope.

The sheep would take baths full of bubbles and soap.

The zebra would put on a dress and a cape,
wear really tall shoes and then dance with an ape.

The tigers would swing among leafy green trees and lazily lounge in the warm summer breeze.

And then they would bake macaroni and cheese.
And say, "Pardon me, but I think I might sneeze!"

And how would the animals celebrate night?
With pj's and milk and a zoo pillow fight!
Feathers would flit! Feathers would float!
Feathers would wake up a sound-asleep goat.

The goat would get mad and throw handfuls of dough,
interrupting a tap-dancing singing pig show.

The pigs, quite surprised at this turn of events,
would scamper and squeal and knock over a fence.

The fence would crash into an all-duck jazz band.

And this is where things would get way out of hand:

The goose would spill juice.

The snakes would all yelp.

The cheetah would pick up the phone and say, "Help!"

Otters would oink!

Chipmunks would chirp!

Rabbits would ribbet and hiccup and burp!

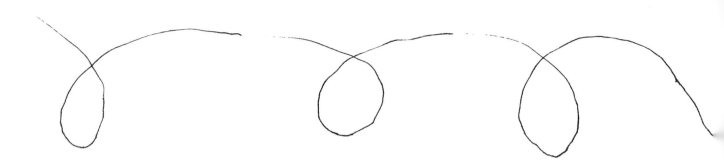

The turtle would trip and land in a pie,
while trying to calm a hysterical fly.

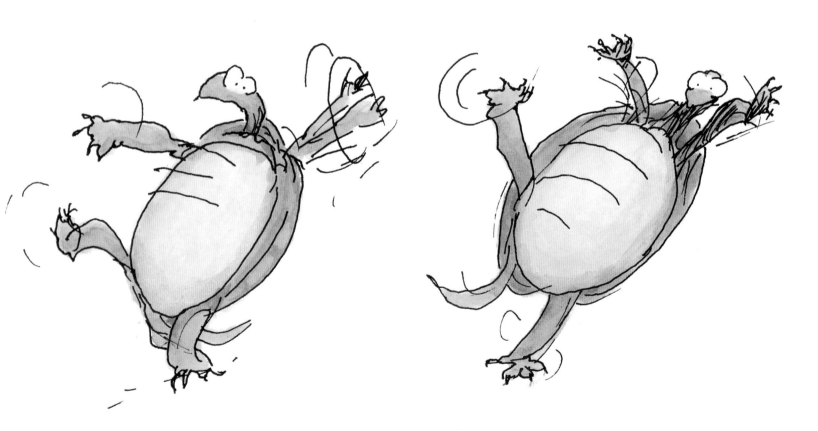

Fish would grab crayons and draw squiggly lines.

Groundhogs would rally and wave protest signs.

Looking around I would quickly assess,
this zoo that I grew was a zoo-rific mess!

So, POOF! I'd take back the juice from the goose,

the dough from the goat,

and the moo from the moose.

And knowing that everything needed to change,
I'd fix all the other things silly and strange.

And then I'd vow never to do THAT again,

until I considered a juggling hen . . .